The Knight who wouldn't Fight

Story by
Helen Docherty

ALISON GREEN BOOKS

Illustrated by
Thomas Docherty

Leo was a gentle knight
In thought and word and deed.
While other knights liked fighting,
Leo liked to sit and read.

He was kind to every creature;
He wouldn't hurt a fly.

When Mum and Dad said,
"Knights must FIGHT!"

He couldn't quite see why.

One morning, Leo's parents said
They'd like to have a chat.
There was nothing wrong with reading,
But he couldn't *just* do that!

They'd seen a lovely advert
In their favourite magazine.
A dragon needed taming!
Leo wasn't very keen.

"Nonsense! You'll enjoy it;
It'll stop you getting bored.
In case the dragon's scary, here's
A brand-new shield and sword."

Leo packed some sandwiches
(And lots of books, of course.)

Then, with a sigh, he saddled up
Old Ned, his faithful horse.

He hadn't travelled far, although
The sun had risen high,
When, suddenly, a fearsome creature
Swooped down from the sky.

It had a lion's body,
But it had an eagle's wings.

"A griffin!" marvelled Leo,
Who had read about such things.

"Come on, then," snarled the griffin,
"I dare you to a fight!"

"I'd rather not," said Leo.
"It wouldn't be quite right.

"I've got my brand-new
sword with me,
So I'd be bound to win it.

"But how about a story
With some pictures
of *you* in it?"

"Yes, please!" the griffin nodded.
(He was really rather vain.)

So Leo read a book to him;
Once – twice –
and then again.

"It's yours to keep," said Leo,
As he clambered back on Ned.
"Oh, thank you!" cried the griffin,
And he bowed his noble head.

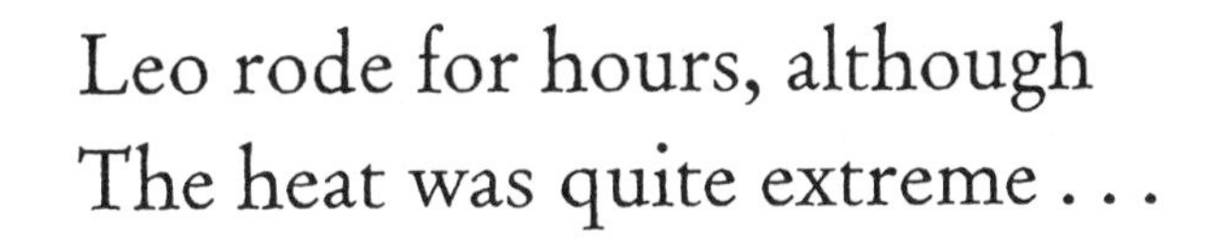

Leo rode for hours, although
The heat was quite extreme . . .

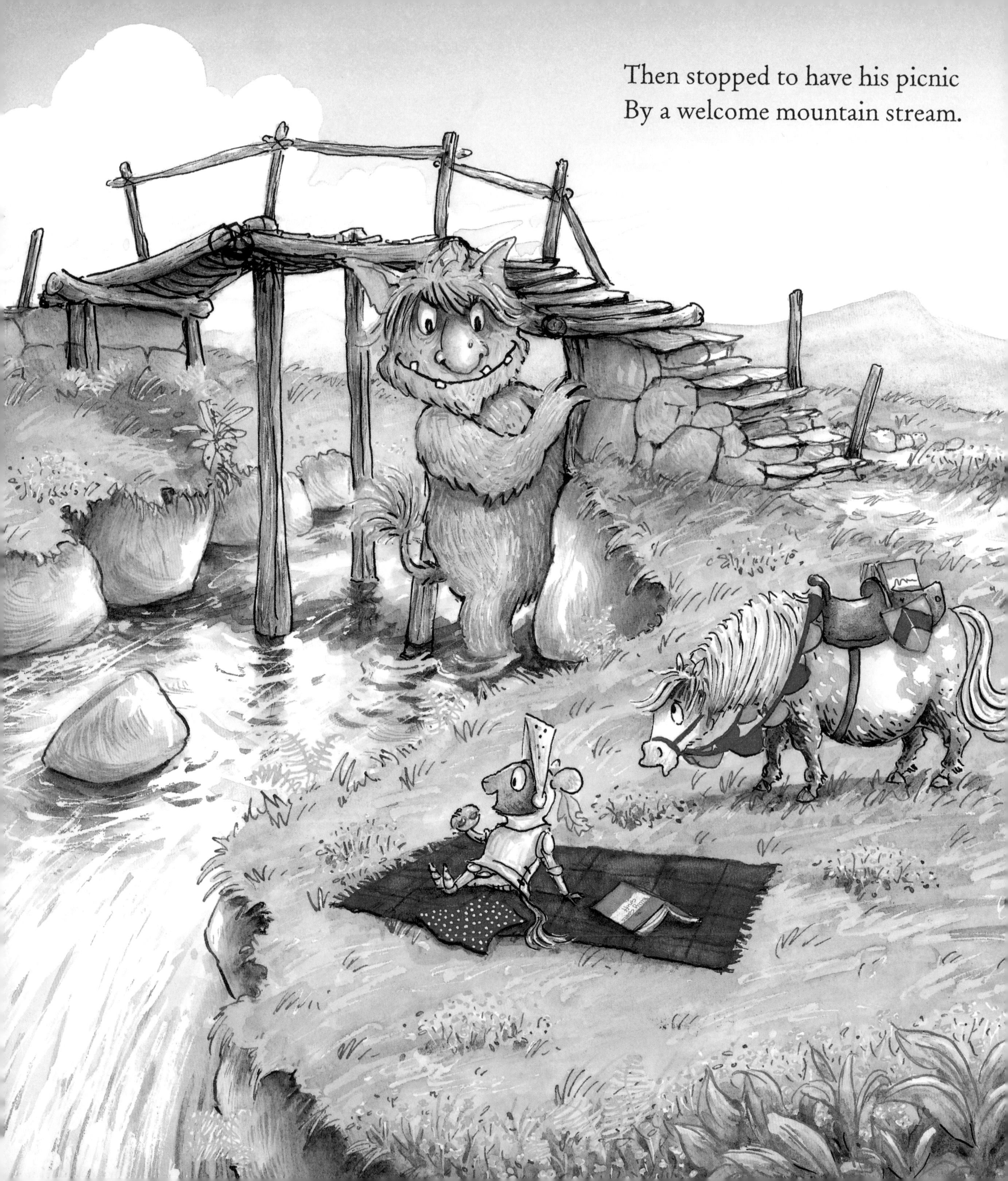

Then stopped to have his picnic
By a welcome mountain stream.

"Who dares to trespass on my bridge?"
Enquired a hungry troll.

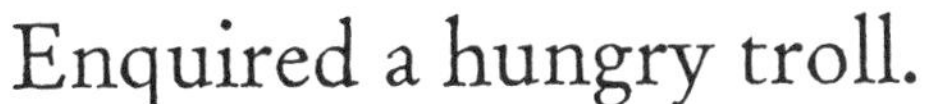

"It's only me," said Leo.
"Would you like to share my roll?"

The troll just laughed.
"No, thanks," he growled.
"I think I'll just eat YOU!"

But Leo said, "My armour's
Pretty difficult to chew.

"I've got a brilliant book, though,
If you'll hang on just a minute . . .
It's full of juicy goats and, look!
It's even got *you* in it."

"Hmm, that sounds good,"
the troll replied,
His hunger put on hold.
So Leo read the story
(With some changes,
truth be told.)

"It's yours to keep," said Leo,
As he clambered back on Ned.
"Oh, thank you!"
cried the grateful troll,
And bowed his heavy head.

Leo kept on riding, through
That long, hot afternoon.
At last, he came upon a town
As empty as the moon.

The leaves were burnt on every tree;
The grass and flowers, too.

And everywhere you looked,
The streets were filled with
dragon poo.

There were faces at the windows –
Folk too scared to go outside.
Leo trotted bravely onwards.
"Hey, watch out!" the people cried.

Then Leo turned a corner
And came nearly nose to nose
With the most ENORMOUS dragon,
Who'd just woken from a doze.

The dragon raised his eyebrows:
"Not another pesky knight!"
"Don't worry!" Leo told him,
"I haven't come to fight.

"I've got the most amazing book,
With loads of dragons in it.

"But it's going in the bin, unless
You clear up right this minute!"

"Oh, don't do that!" the dragon cried,
"I'll clean it up right now!
But I'm really bad at tidying.
Perhaps you'll show me how?"

So Leo taught the dragon
How to shovel,
scoop and clear.

And, one by one, the townsfolk
All began to lose their fear.

“Now can I have my story?”
Begged the dragon,
on his knees.

So Leo read the book six times.
(A dragon’s hard to please.)

"It's yours to keep," said Leo,
As he clambered back on Ned.
"Oh, thank you," cried the dragon,
And he bowed his scaly head.

WELCOME
HOME,
LEO

When Leo reached his home at last,
The cheers were long and loud.
His parents hugged him very tight.
"Well done! You've made us proud."

Now Leo is a hero,
His parents have agreed . . .

The Billy Goats uff
MOUSE TALES

He doesn't have to fight at all.
He's left in peace – to read.

For Helen's dad, Gareth (another gentle knight), and for our very own Leo.
Also for Wilf, Felix, Laurie, Jake, Max and Edward.

First published in the UK in 2016 by
Alison Green Books
An imprint of Scholastic Children's Books
Euston House, 24 Eversholt Street
London NW1 1DB
A division of Scholastic Ltd
www.scholastic.co.uk
London – New York – Toronto – Sydney – Auckland
Mexico City – New Delhi – Hong Kong

HB ISBN: 978 1 407163 25 3
PB ISBN: 978 1 407163 48 2

Printed in Malaysia

1 3 5 7 9 8 6 4 2

Papers used by Scholastic Children's Books are made from wood grown in sustainable forests.